W9-BUY-396

THE COURAGEOUS
CAPTAIN
AMERICA™

AN ORIGIN STORY

Based on the Marvel comic book series **Captain America**

Adapted by Rich Thomas

Interior Illustrated by Val Semeiks, Bob McLeod,
Hi-Fi Design, *and* The Storybook Art Group

New York

visit us at www.abdopublishing.com

Reinforced library bound edition published in 2013 by Spotlight, a division of the ABDO Group, PO Box 398166, Minneapolis, MN 55439. Spotlight produces high-quality reinforced library bound editions for schools and libraries. Published by agreement with Marvel Press, an imprint of Disney Book Group, LLC.

Printed in the United States of America, North Mankato, Minnesota.
042012
052013
♲ This book contains at least 10% recycled materials.

For Duke
—RT

TM & © 2012 Marvel & Subs.

All Rights Reserved. No part of this book may be reproduced or transmitted in any form or by any means, electronic or mechanical, including photocopying, recording, or by any information storage and retrieval system, without written permission from the publisher.

Library of Congress Cataloging-in-Publication Data

This book was previously cataloged with the following information:
Thomas, Richard.
The courageous Captain America origin storybook / [edited by] Richard Thomas.
p. cm.
1. America, Captain (Fictitious character)—Juvenile fiction. 2. Superheroes—Juvenile fiction. I. Title.
PZ7.T36933 2012
[E]-dc223

2010938845

ISBN 978-1-61479-008-2 (reinforced library edition)

All Spotlight books are reinforced library binding and manufactured in the United States of America.

Before you were born—in fact, long before even the oldest person you know had been born—a peaceful little island sat right off the mainland of a place that was called different things by all the different nations of people who lived there.

As time went on,

more and more people came
to this **little island.**

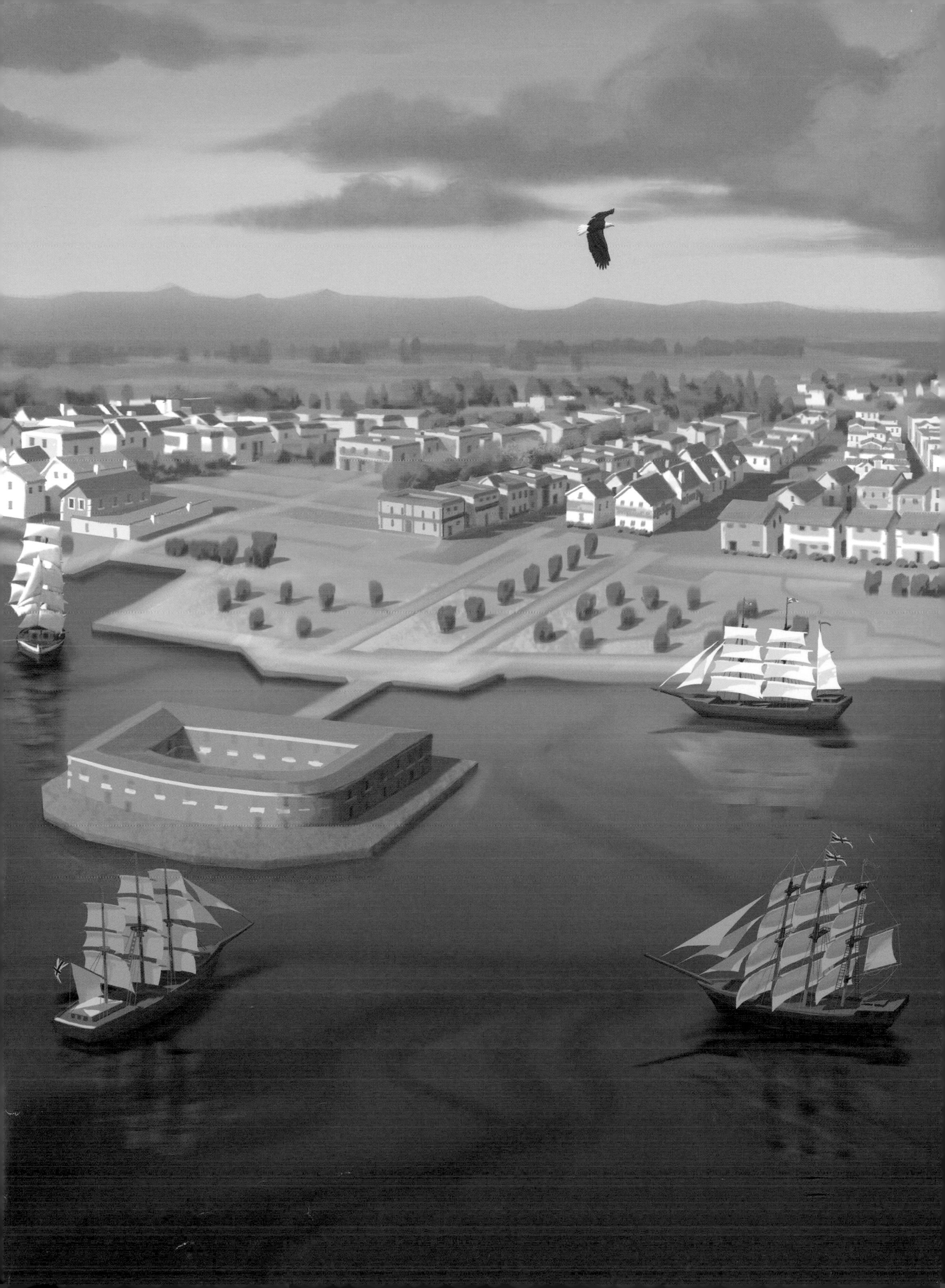

They wanted to leave behind the lives they led
in a place they called the **Old World**

and build new ones in a place where they
believed **anything was possible**.

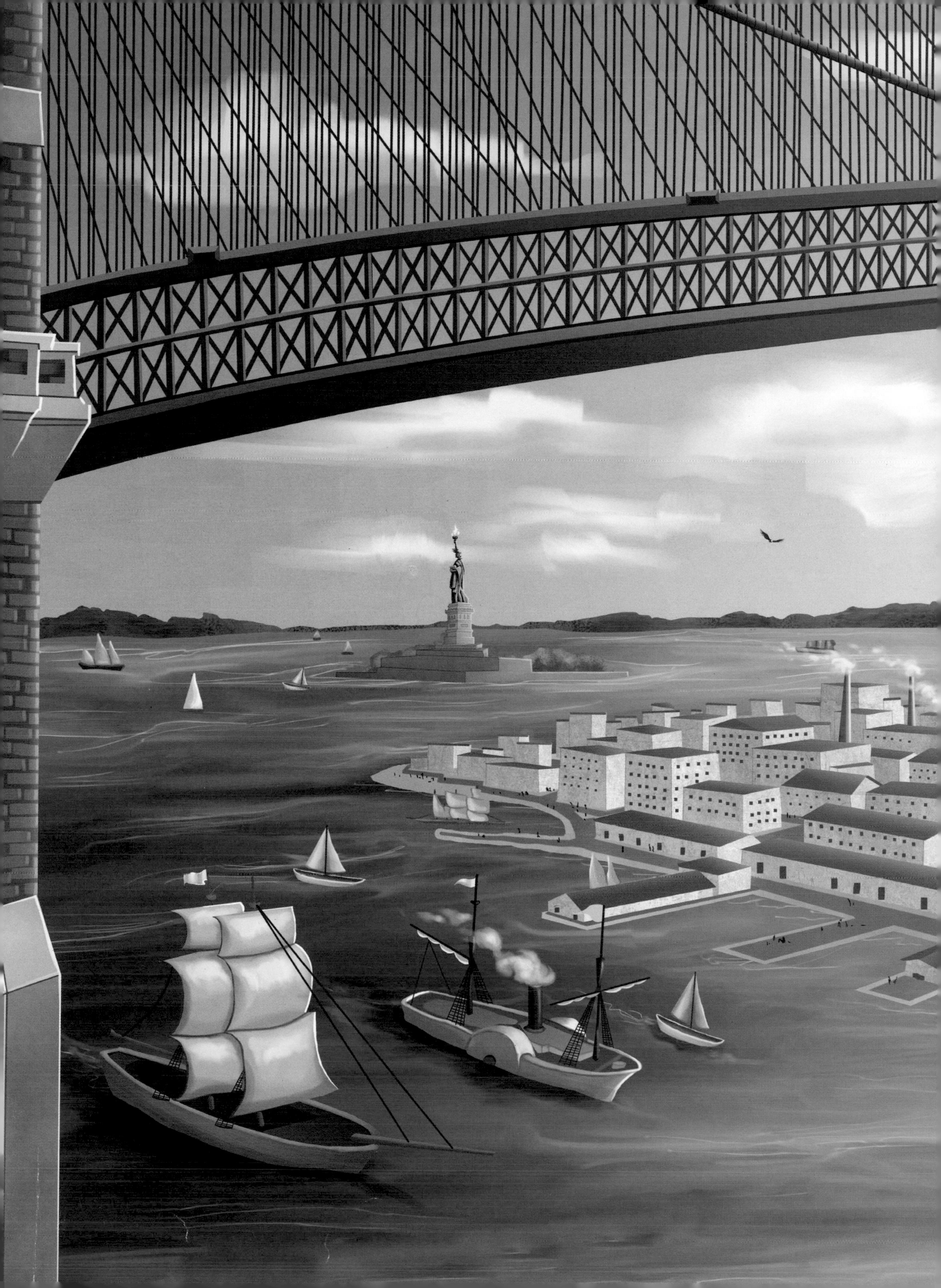

They came from all over the world.

For most, this island was the
first stop on the path to a
new life in this young nation.

This island was known as Manhattan, in **the city of New York.**

The country would be known as the United States of America—

or *America,* for short.

Before America was even two hundred years old,

it was called upon to fight alongside other countries in a **terrible war** that was destroying the world.

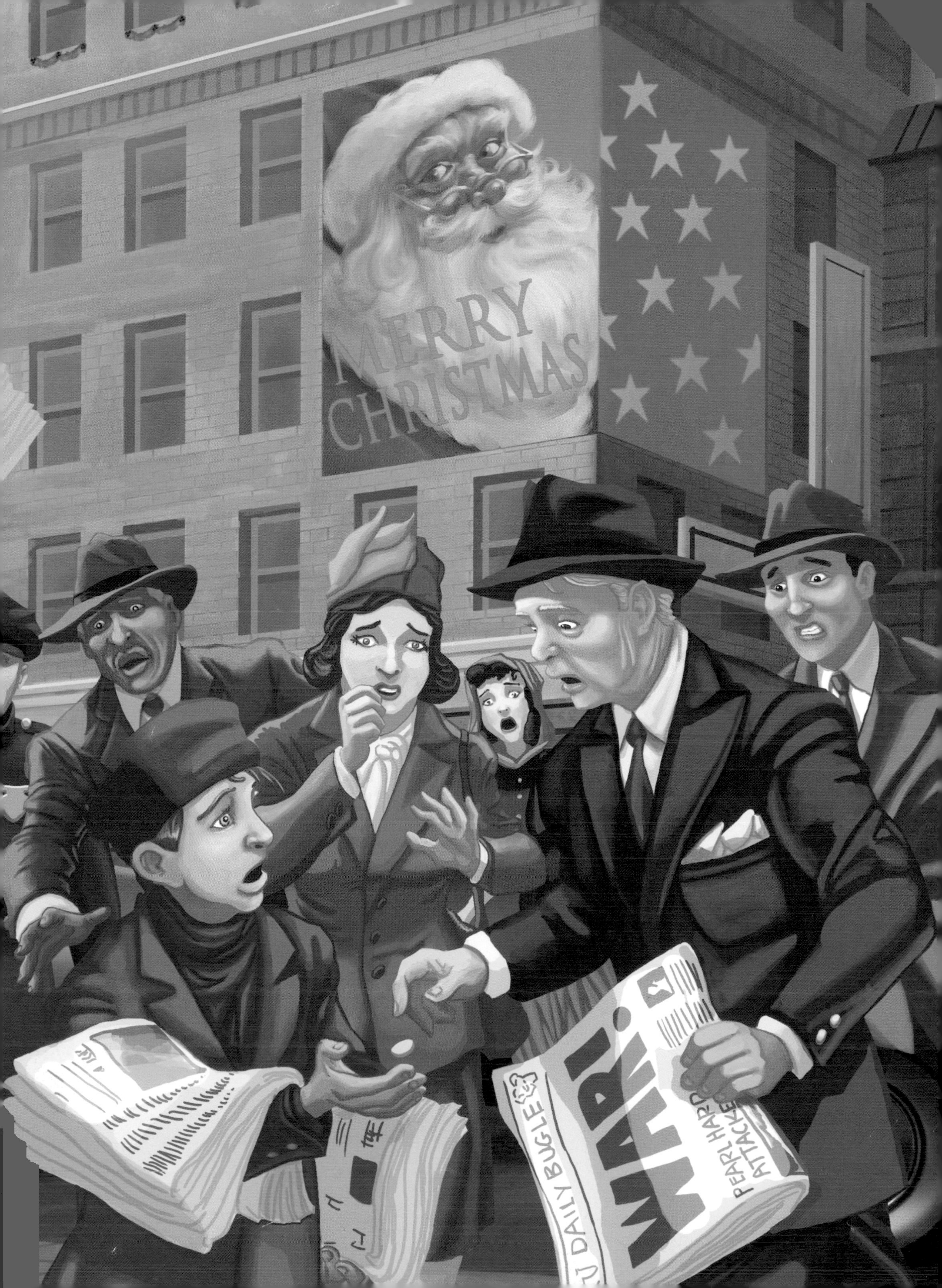
MERRY CHRISTMAS
DAILY BUGLE
WAR!
PEARL HAR
ATTACKE

The news of war moved people.

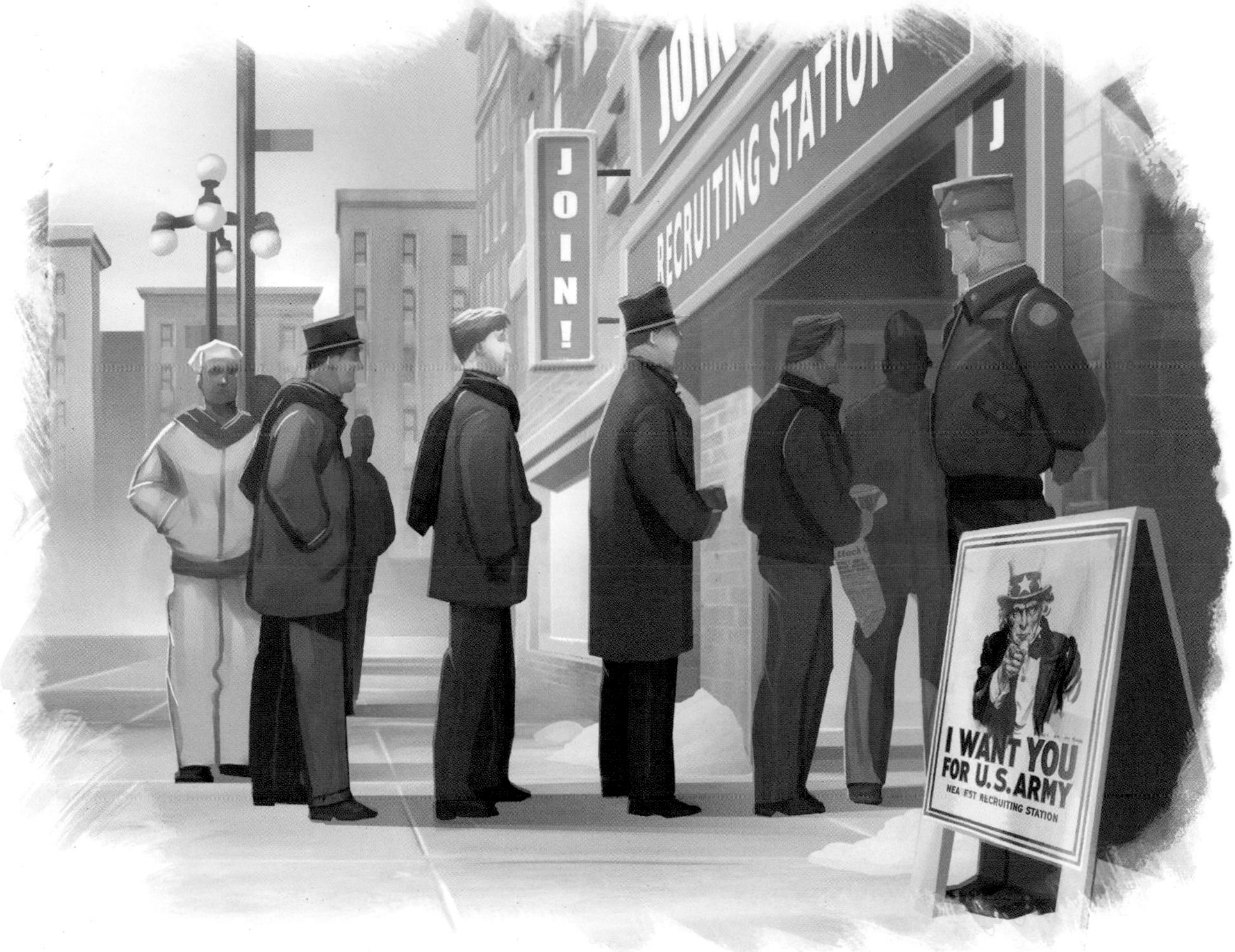
RECRUITING STATION
JOIN!
I WANT YOU
FOR U.S.ARMY

It seemed like everyone
in the country wanted
to join the army
to **help.**

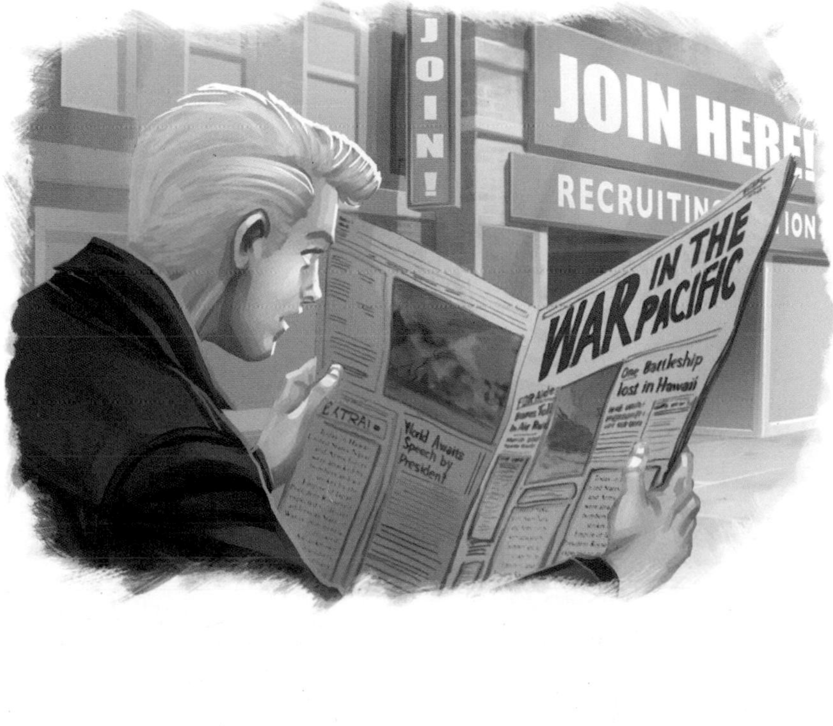
JOIN!
WAR IN THE PACIFIC
One Battleship lost in Hawaii
EXTRA!
World Awaits Speech by President

Including a young man named **Steve Rogers**.

Steve had been upset about the
war for some time. Now that
America was involved, he could
do something about it.

Soon, Steve was on a long line
of men waiting to be examined.
If the men passed, they would
be deployed to the war.

Steve waited his turn.

Every man so far had passed.

Steve was **confident** he would, too.

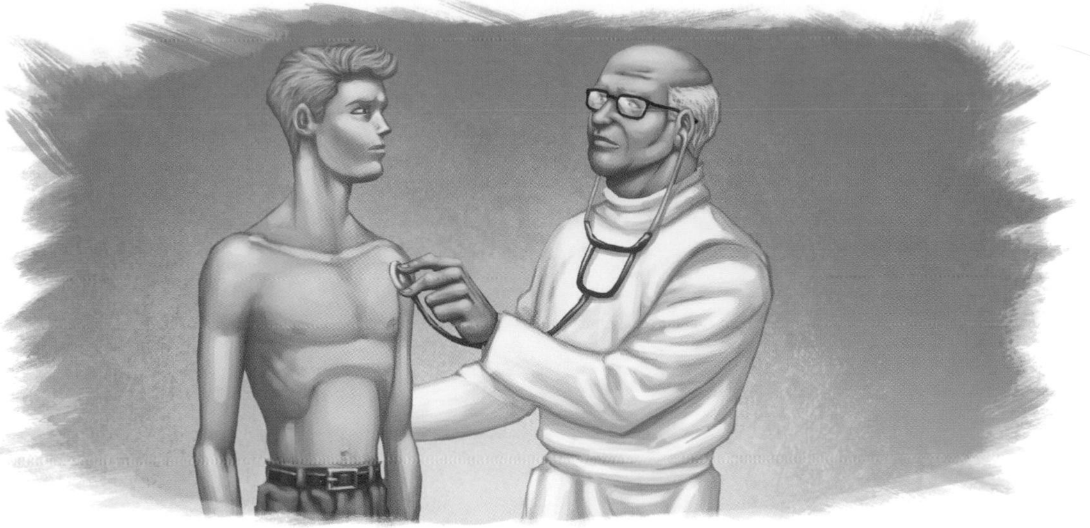

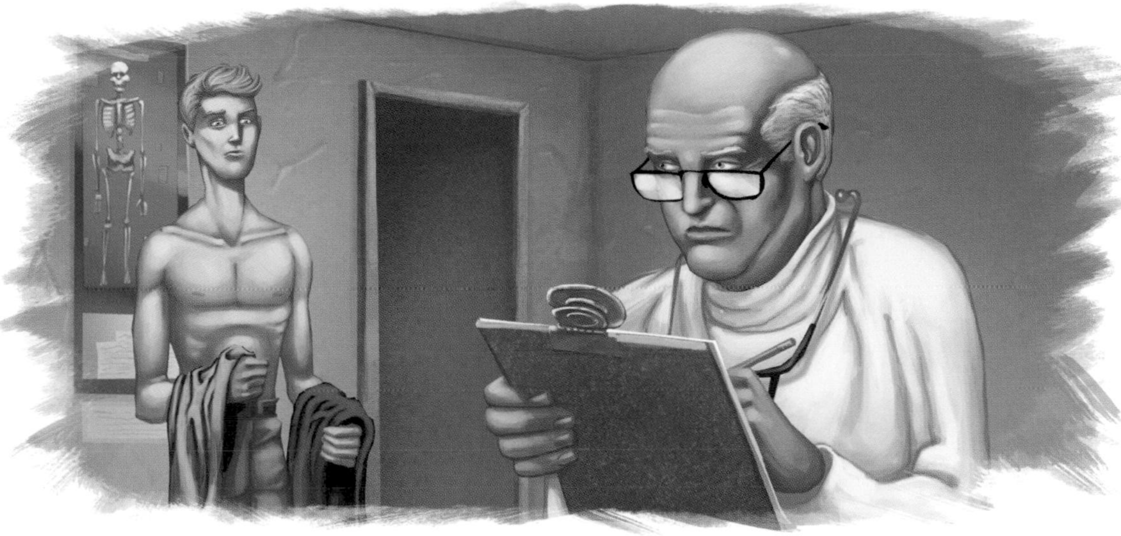

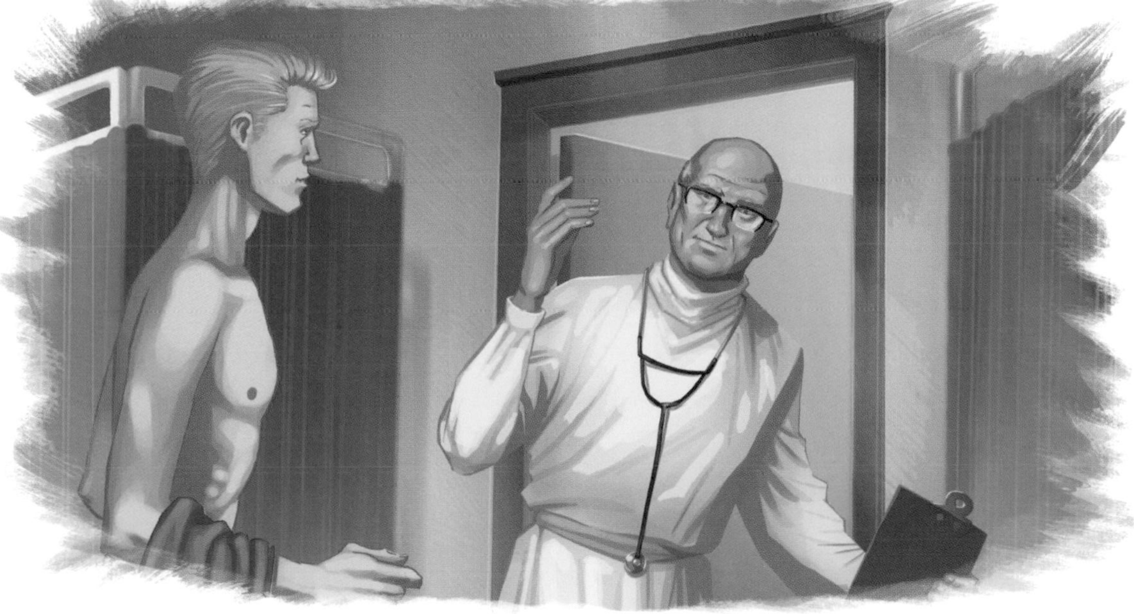

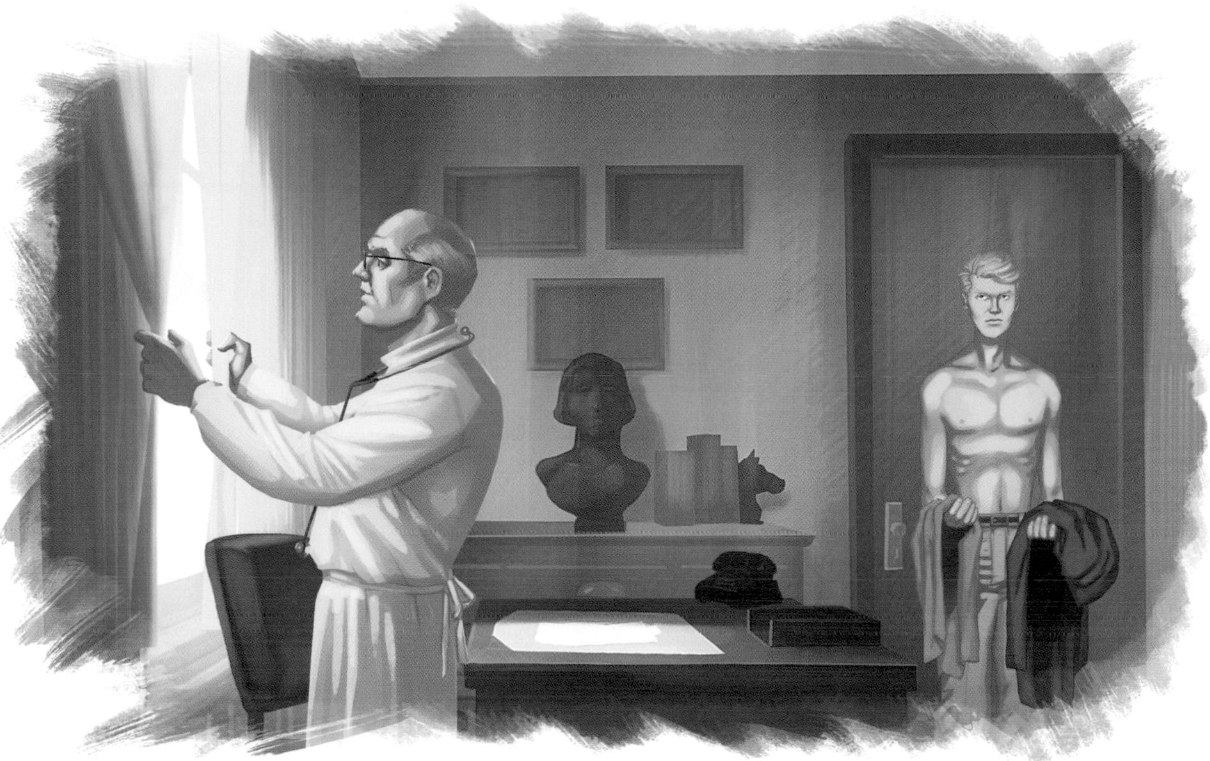

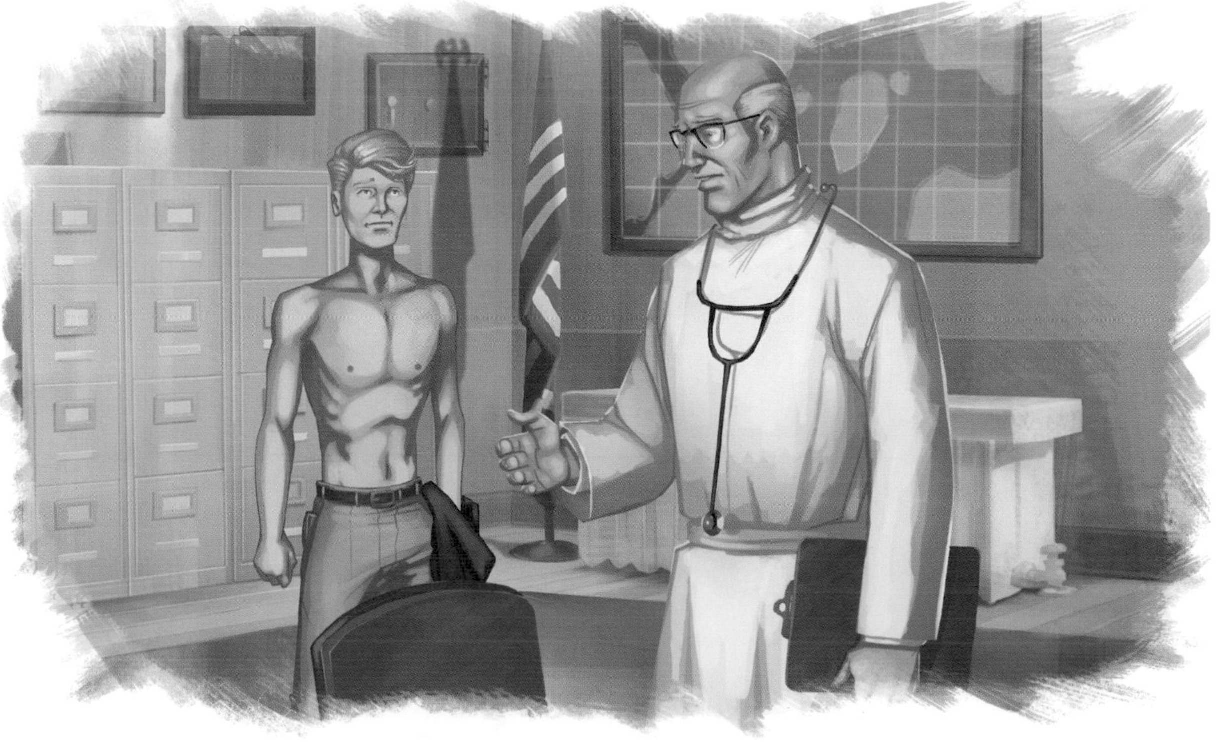

The doctor told Steve that he
was in no shape to join
the army.

But then he told him there was another way to get
into the army. He handed Steve a file marked

CLASSIFIED—PROJECT: REBIRTH.

The doctor told Steve that if the experiment worked,
he would be able to join the army.

Steve said he would try anything to become a soldier.

The doctor called in a general named **Chester Phillips**.
General Phillips was in charge of Project: Rebirth.

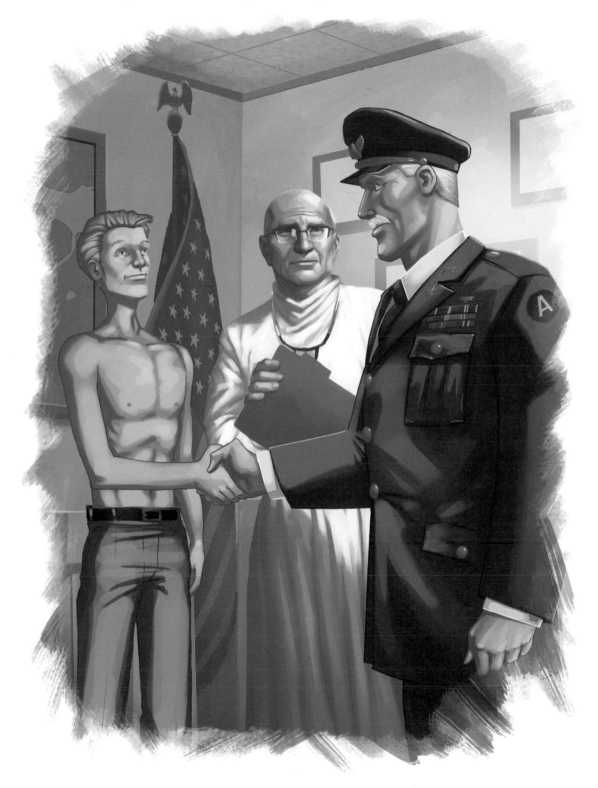

The general led Steve down a **hidden hallway** to a secret exit.

Soon the two men were crossing the bridge into nearby Brooklyn.

They arrived at an antiques shop in a run-down, dangerous-looking area.

An **old woman** let them in and led them downstairs.

But the storefront was not an antiques shop at all!
It was a cover for an **underground lab**.

And the owner was not an old woman,
but a **secret agent!**

General Phillips introduced Steve to the
project's lead scientist, **Doctor Erskine**.

He told Steve that the **Super-Soldier serum** . . .

. . . combined with the **Vita-Rays** . . .

...would transform him
from frail and sickly...

...into America's

FIRST AVENGER!

The experiment was a

SUCCESS!

But before Steve, General Phillips, or anyone else in the lab could notice, an **enemy spy** who had been working in the lab attacked!

He did not want the Americans to have such power!

The doctor was hurt and unable to duplicate the serum.

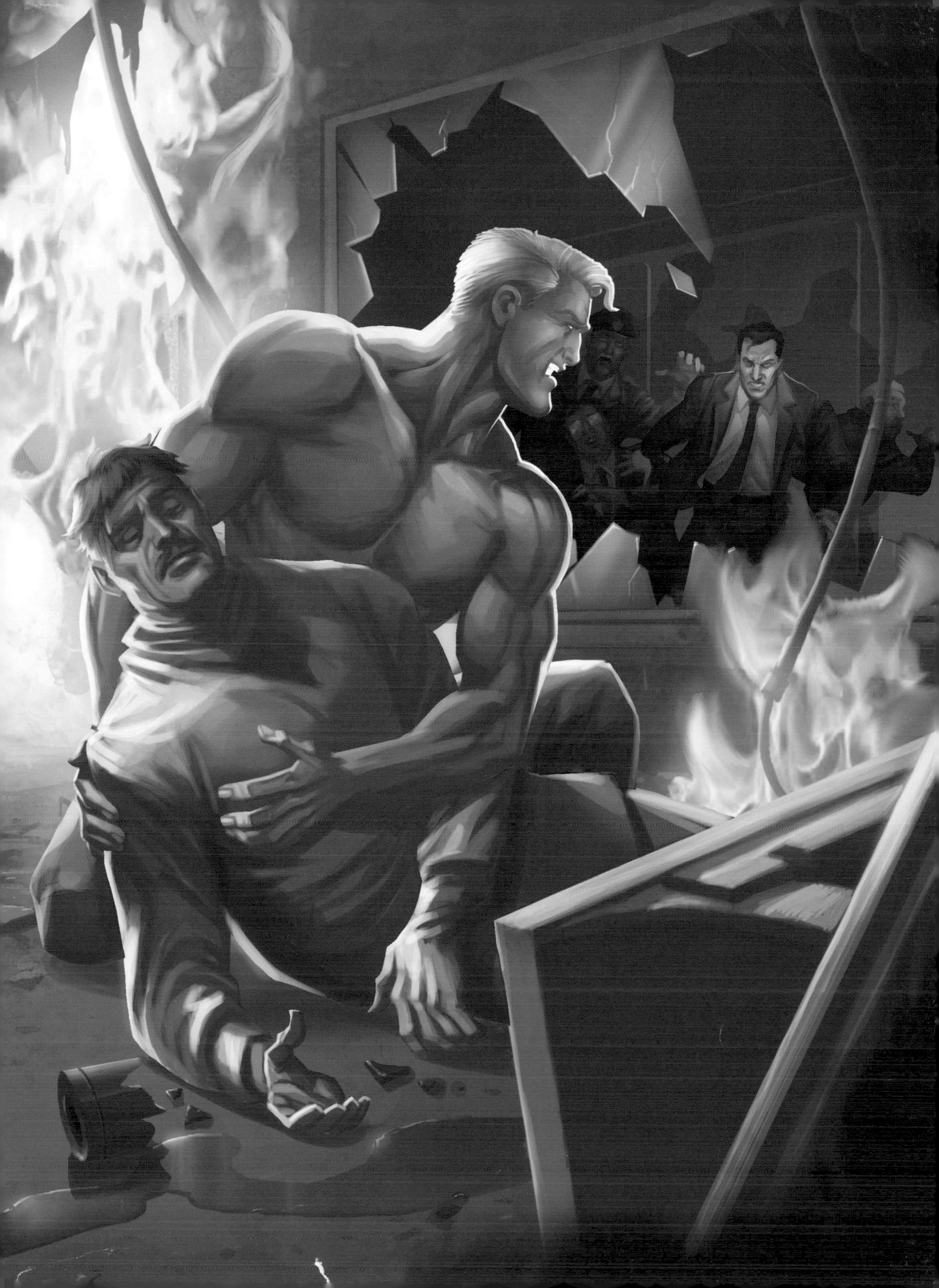

But Steve, in his new Super-Soldier body, was safe.

AND HE WAS ANGRY!

The army put Steve through a very
special training camp to teach him how
to use his new body.

The general presented Steve with a **special shield** made of the strongest metal known and a **unique costume** to help Steve mask his identity.

With the costume and shield, Steve would now be known as America's most powerful soldier . . .

CAPTAIN AMERICA!

Captain America's missions were often **dangerous**.

In order to keep his secret safe, the general asked Steve to pretend to be a **clumsy** army private.

But when no one was looking, Steve donned his costume and fought for **justice**.

Steve's reputation as a klutz meant he was transferred often.

But Steve's moving around allowed **Captain America** to fight on many different fronts of the worldwide war!

No one ever suspected that the worst private in the US Army

was also the **best soldier** that the army had.

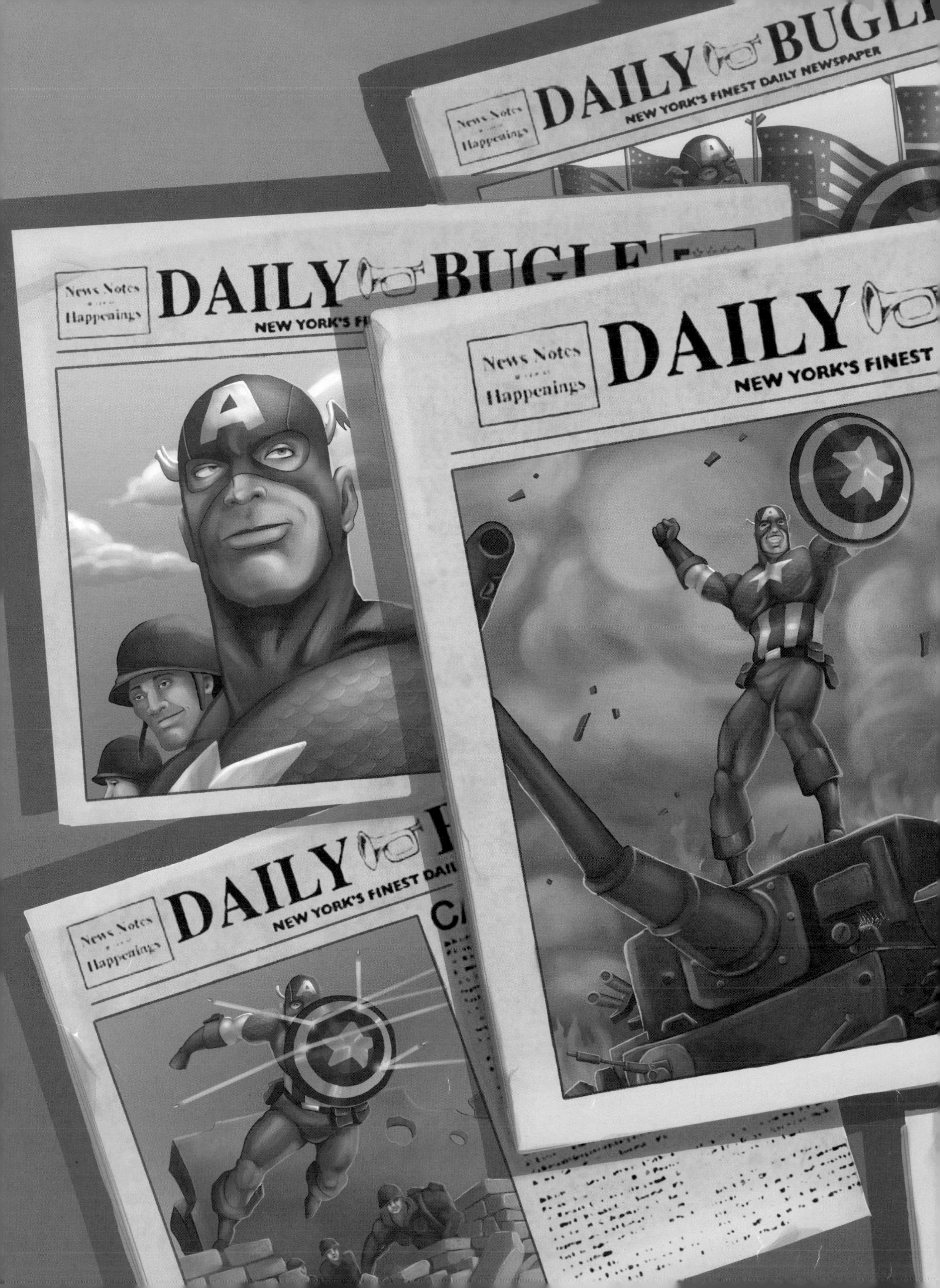

DAILY BUGLE
NEW YORK'S FINEST DAILY NEWSPAPER
News Notes
Happenings
DAILY BUGLE
NEW YORK'S FI
News Notes
Happenings
DAILY
NEW YORK'S FINEST
News Notes
Happenings
DAILY
NEW YORK'S FINEST DAIL
News Notes
Happenings

BUGLE
ILY NEWSPAPER

FINAL

TANK NO MATCH FOR CAP!

CAP RECEIVES HIGHEST HONOR

Captain America kept on fighting
for **liberty**, until finally...

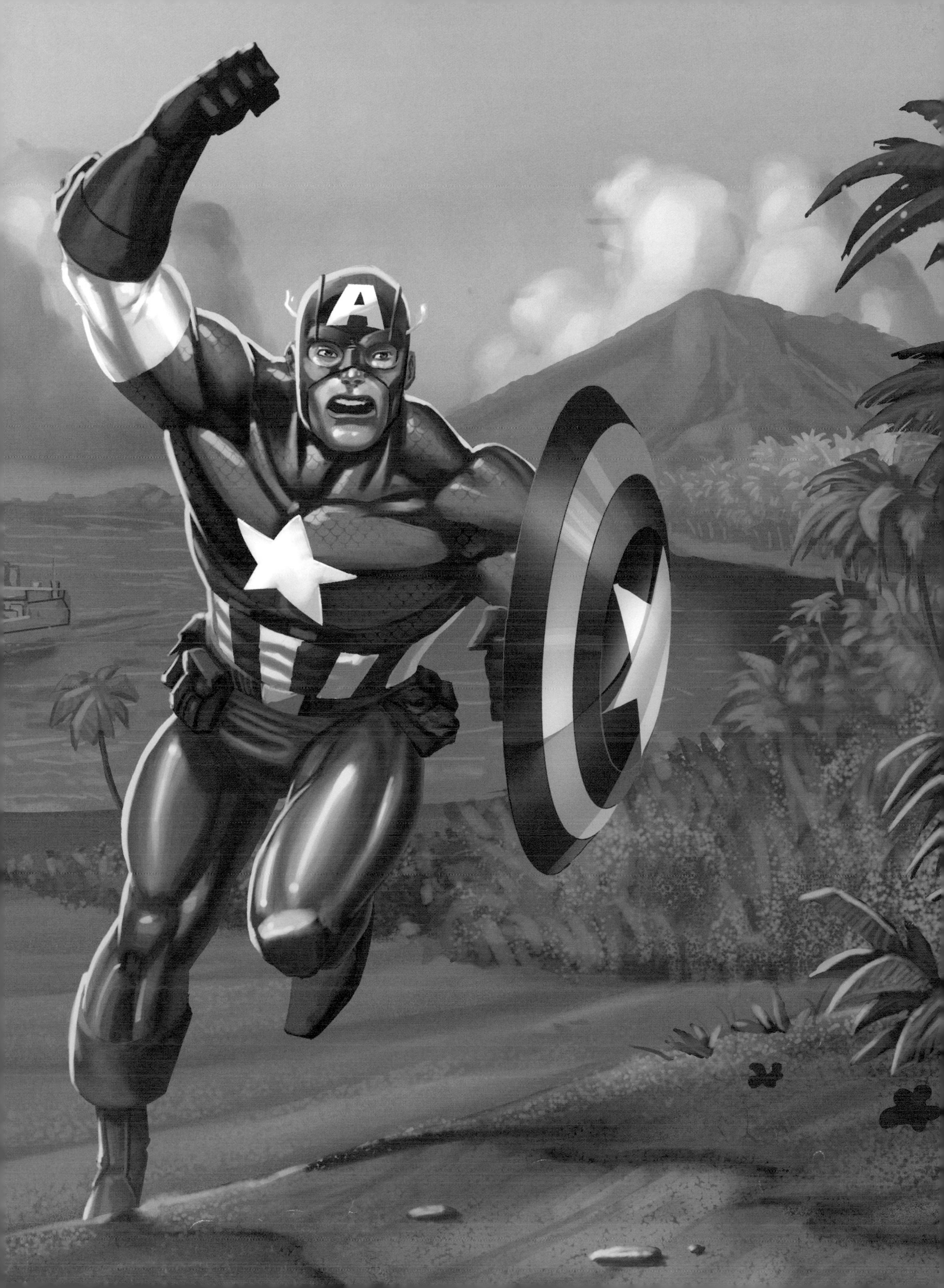

THE WAR HAD BEEN WON.

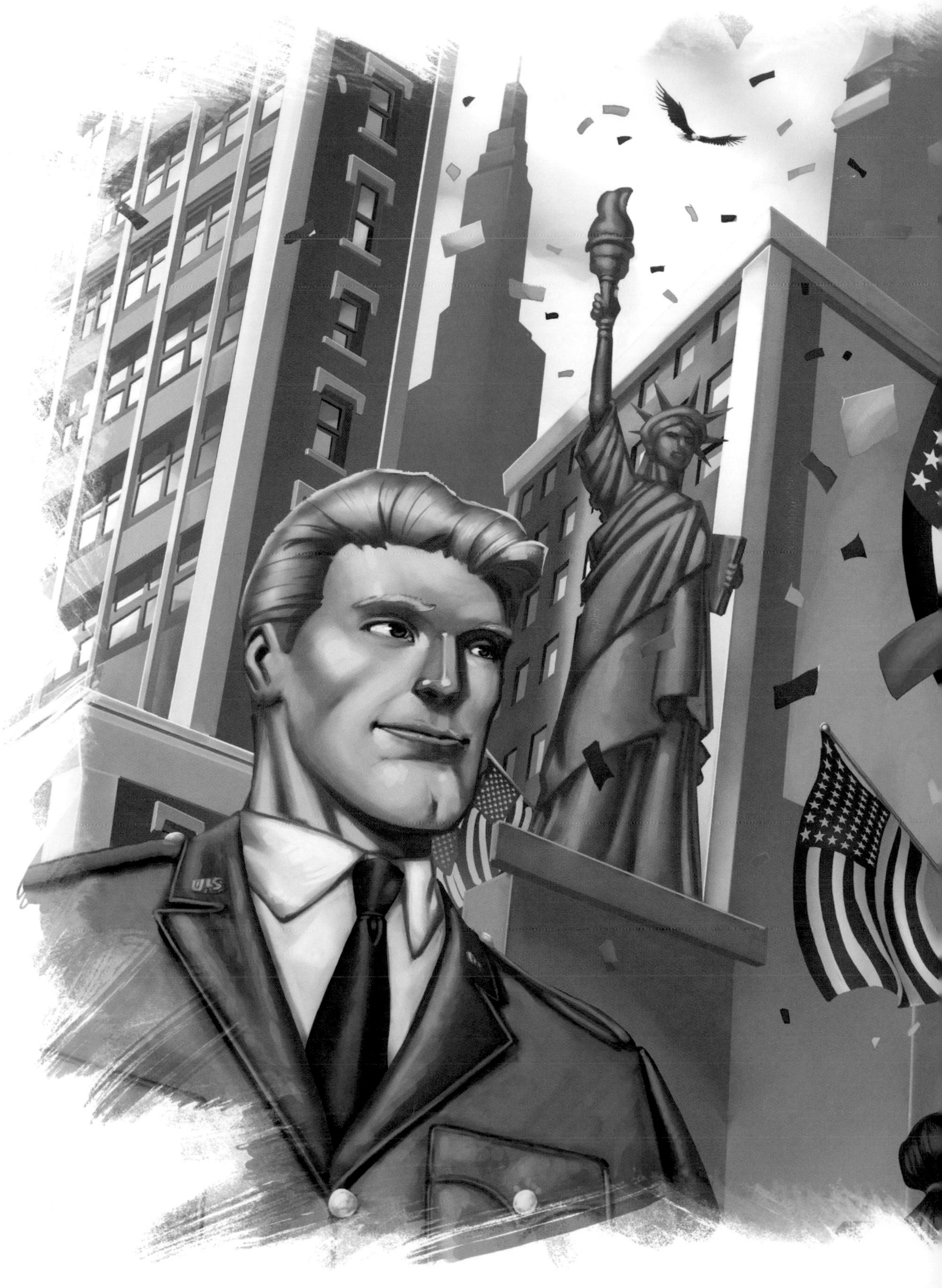

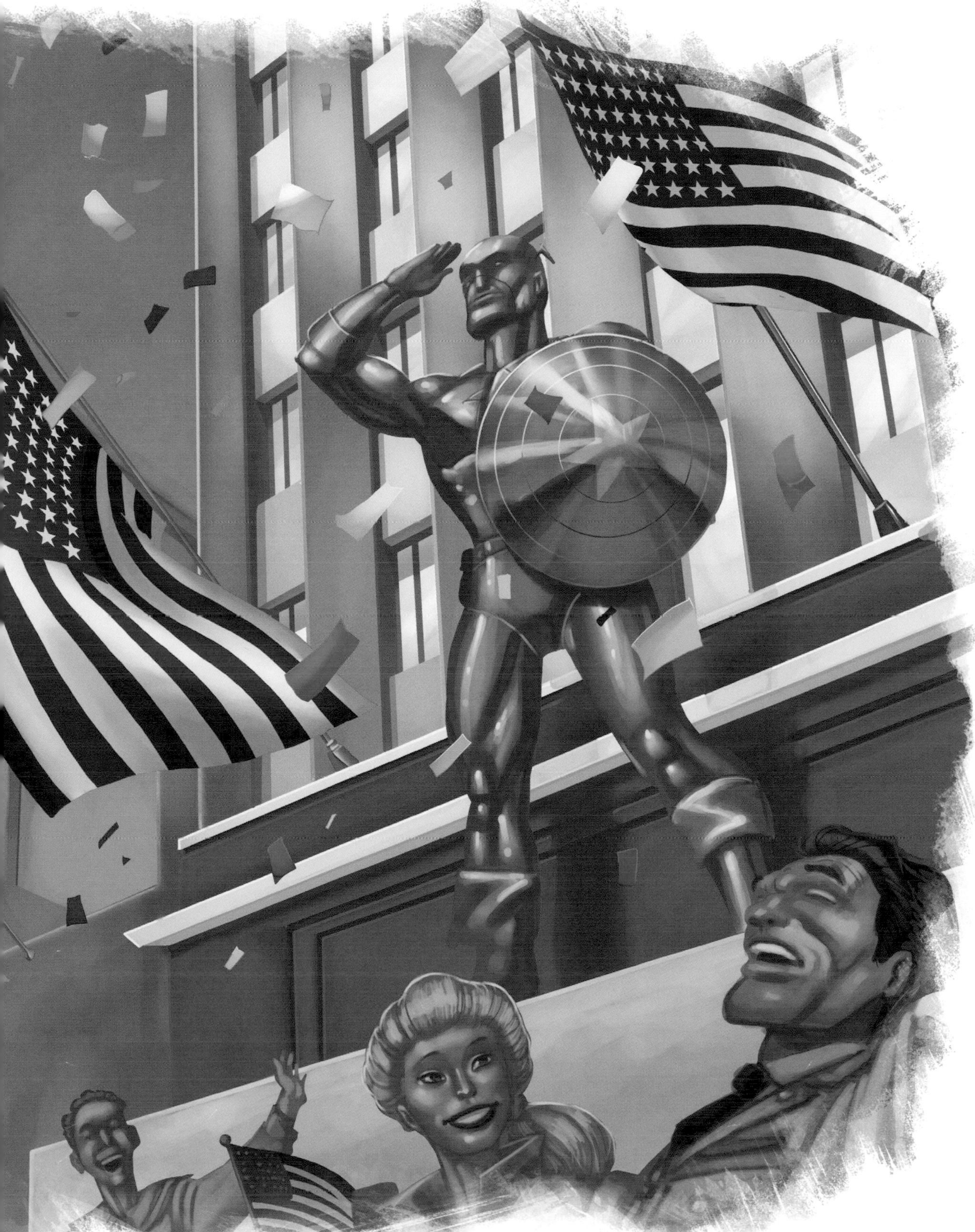

Though the country might not
always live up to its promises,
as long as Steve was able, he
vowed to protect it and its ideals:
justice, equality, freedom...

THE
ORIGINAL
NEW
YORKERS

. . .and the dream of what the nation
he loved could accomplish.

FREDERICK COUNTY PUBLIC LIBRARIES   OCT   2018   21982318736521

FREDERICK COUNTY PUBLIC LIBRARIES   OCT   2018   21982318736521